T0001792

MAD for MATH

BECOME A MONSTER AT MATHEMATICS!

EDITED BY LINDA BERTOLA

ILLUSTRATIONS BY AGNESE BARUZZI

WSkids
WHITE STAR KIDS

Dragon Fruit

TO START...

LEARNING MATH BY HAVING FUN IS NOT ONLY POSSIBLE, IT IS NECESSARY, EVEN AT A YOUNG AGE.

This book offers activities and chances to approach the world of numbers in a captivating, motivating way that also facilitates a positive attitude towards math.

Pedagogical studies have shown how the motivation at the base of long-lasting learning is linked to enjoyment: this is why we have chosen a playful approach. Playing fosters intuition and the acquisition of fundamental mathematical concepts.

The distinctive setting and the guide-characters leading the child reinforce positive participation. Each chapter begins with a short story that links the mathematical tasks to a "reality," even if it is an imaginary one. Moreover, this narrative approach stimulates children's curiosity.

Topics are presented in a gradual, intuitive way. We have chosen an inductive approach, therefore concepts are never formalized—we have not given any definitions or used specific terminology.

We have also proposed some easy "do-it-yourself" ideas that can be made with common materials or with something included in the book, to foster learning through a creative-tactile approach.

THIS BOOK IS AIMED AT CHILDREN IN GRADE 1 TO 2.

CONTENT:

- Counting up to 20
- Comparing and ordering numbers
- Addition and subtraction
- Multiplication as a repeated addition
- Introduction to the concept of division
- Problems

SOME ADVICE FOR THE ADULTS:

Respect children's timing and their "refusals"! If they close the book or skip a page, it doesn't mean they are giving up. Maybe they just need to quietly process their thinking.

Ask questions, don't give answers! If your child asks for help, don't tell him or her the answer. Ask targeted questions to help them understand the task or the mistake they made.

Let children find their own way, even if it's a long, twisted one. You could then help them explore other roads and maybe find the more clever one to reach the solution.

The first step is solving and understanding. Help children elaborate their thoughts, by asking them to explain verbally or by drawing or using tangible materials in the proposed setting before trying to find a solution or calculation: that's the easiest and least fun part!

Ask "How did you do that?" Gradually get them used to explaining their reasoning: knowing how I reflected and why is much more important than the name of the rule I applied.

The settings proposed in this book are obviously born from our imagination. You can help children retrace numbers and math in their daily lives. Get out of the book and meet math!

WELCOME TO ZOT!

Maybe you don't know this, but in a far away corner of the universe there is a small kingdom named ZOT.

There are houses, shops, offices and schools in Zot. The streets are full of traffic and cars in rush hour, and there are children and elderly people, policewomen and male teachers, artists and pilots.

What? You think it's like any other kingdom? Well, not at all:

ZOT IS INHABITED BY MONSTERS!

There are huge and tiny monsters, some as spiky as needles and others as sticky as jelly. They have antennae or tentacles and a different number of arms and legs. We can really say they suit all tastes.

You also need to know that these monsters aren't really as meek as lambs: there are clumsy monsters and pranksters, crabby monsters and trouble-makers. So, as you can imagine, they are really up to all sorts of things in Zot.

IF YOU WANT TO FIND OUT MORE, YOU JUST NEED TO START READING THIS BOOK AND HAVE... TREMENDOUS FUN!

CONNECT THE DOTS!

DISCOVER SOME OF THE MONSTERS LIVING IN THE KINGDOM OF ZOT, THEN COLOR THEM IN AS YOU PLEASE.

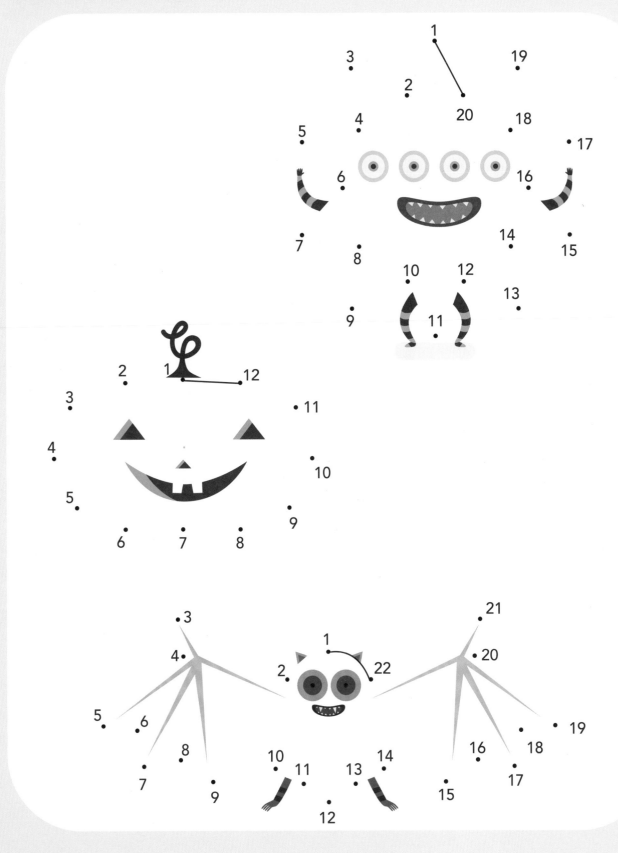

HERE ARE SOME OF ZOT'S INHABITANTS.

COMPLETE THEIR IDS: FIND BIT BOT'S AND ZIG ZAG'S PICTURES AMONG THE STICKERS.

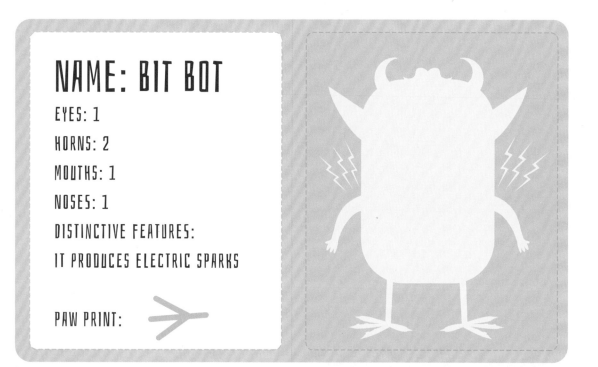

NAME: BIT BOT

EYES: 1

HORNS: 2

MOUTHS: 1

NOSES: 1

DISTINCTIVE FEATURES:

IT PRODUCES ELECTRIC SPARKS

PAW PRINT:

NAME: ZIG ZAG

EYES: 2

NOSES: 0

MOUTHS: 1

LEGS: 4

DISTINCTIVE FEATURES:

IT LOVES TO DANCE

PAW PRINT:

WRITE THE MISSING INFORMATION ON THESE IDS AND INVENT GLUX'S ONE.

NAME: MOLLY

EYES: _____

ANTENNAE: _____

MOUTHS: _____

NOSES: _____

DISTINCTIVE FEATURES: IT CAN BOUNCE

PAW PRINT:

NAME: SPYX

_____ : 3

_____ : 0

_____ : 6

_____ : 1

DISTINCTIVE FEATURES: IT'S WEARING A HAT WITH A POMPOM

PAW PRINT:

NAME: GLUX

EYES: _____

TENTACLES: _____

TEETH: _____

NOSES: _____

DISTINCTIVE FEATURES: IT'S A SKILLED SWIMMER AND VERY SLIMY

PAW PRINT:

IT'S REALLY CROWDED AT RUSH HOUR!

THERE ARE MONSTERS GOING TO WORK, MONSTERS GOING SHOPPING, MONSTERS GOING TO SCHOOL OR AT THE PARK.

COUNT THE MONSTERS AND COMPLETE:

MONSTERS IN TOTAL:_____

MONSTERS THAT ARE NOT BLUE:_____

RED MONSTERS:_____

MONSTERS WITH ONE EYE: _____

FURRY MONSTERS:_____

MONSTERS WITH MORE THAN 2 EYES: _____

MONSTERS WITHOUT ANTENNAE:_____

GO AROUND THE CITY.

FOLLOW THE INSTRUCTIONS AND COLOR THE WINDOWS.

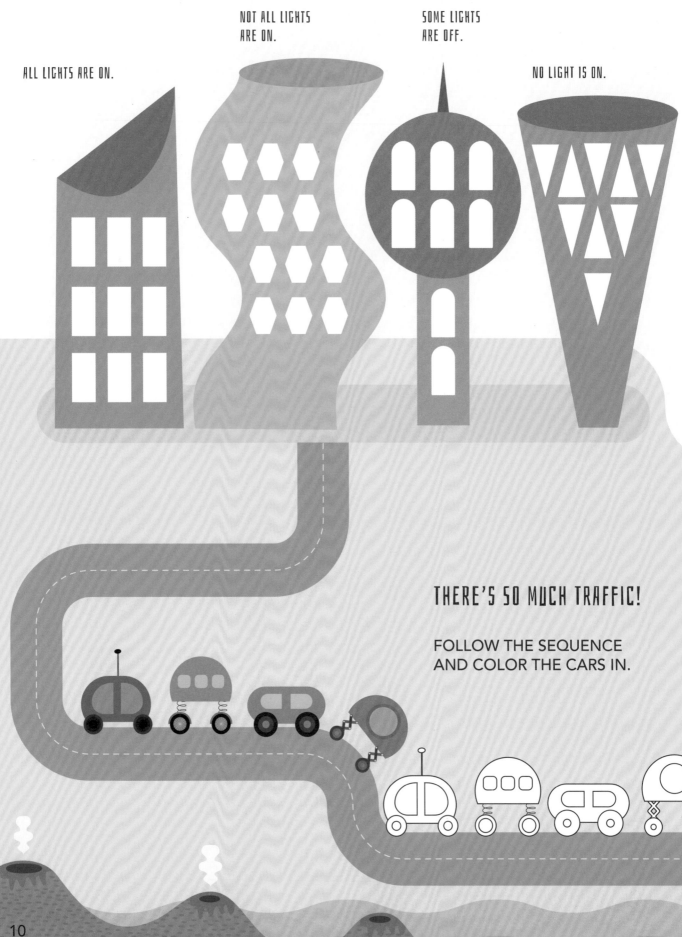

NOT ALL LIGHTS ARE ON.

SOME LIGHTS ARE OFF.

ALL LIGHTS ARE ON.

NO LIGHT IS ON.

THERE'S SO MUCH TRAFFIC!

FOLLOW THE SEQUENCE AND COLOR THE CARS IN.

MAKE ZOT'S SKYSCRAPERS APPEAR!

COLOR IN THE SQUARES AS INDICATED, LIKE IN THE EXAMPLES.

5	7	10	11	8	7	9	11	6	10	11

THE MYSTERY OF THE MISSING SNACKS

Every day of every month of every year, at exactly 4:27 pm, it's snack time in Zot. When the clock says it's snack time, all monsters stop whatever they're doing and take their snacks out.

Therefore, it may happen that you are left on the dentist's chair with your mouth still open, or that the barber goes away just after putting shaving cream on your face. Matches are put on hold, all chores are stopped: there's nothing more important than having a snack for a truly respectful monster.

The greediest have a rich four-course meal at snack time, and let's not talk about those lucky ones who have two or more mouths and numerous arms that allow them to enjoy a lot of delicacies at the same time.

BUT SOMETHING STRANGE HAPPENED TODAY!

The sound of the bell indicating it was snack time wasn't followed by the clink-clacking of cutlery and plates, nor by the typical paper rustle that follows this afternoon snack.

After a moment of complete silence, all we could see were monsters running about in all directions, desperate because their snacks had disappeared. That's right: every basket, tin or packet in the whole kingdom was completely empty!

A mystery to solve for the detective monster who, in the blink of an eye, found the loot by following the tracks the clumsy thief had left. The culprit was none other than the greedy monster, who thought he could manage to stock up food.

Luckily, it all worked out in the end and all monsters got their snacks back.

THE SNACK THIEF HAS LEFT SOME TRACKS. FOLLOW THESE CHOCOLATE
FOOTPRINTS BY CONNECTING THEM IN AN ASCENDING ORDER.

COMPLETE THE LABELS!

THE SNACKS HAVE BEEN ARRANGED SO THAT THEY CAN BE GIVEN BACK TO THEIR OWNERS. COMPLETE THEM WITH THE CORRECT NUMBERS.

| 0 | 1 | | | | | |

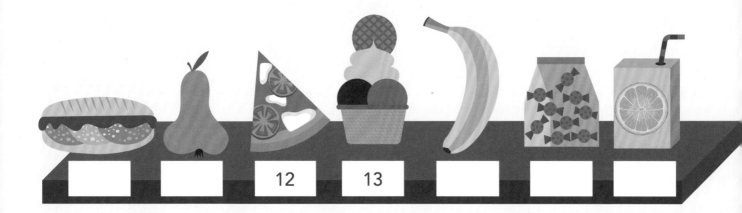

| | | 12 | 13 | | | |

| | 6 | 5 | | | | |

PILES AND PILES OF SNACKS HAVE BEEN FOUND IN THE GREEDY MONSTER'S PANTRY... WRITE THE NUMBER OF ELEMENTS AND COLOR THEM IN BY FOLLOWING THE INSTRUCTIONS.

COLOR THE PILE WITH THE BIGGEST QUANTITY.

 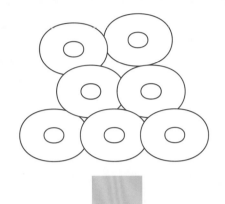 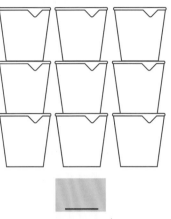

COLOR THE PILE WITH THE SMALLEST QUANTITY.

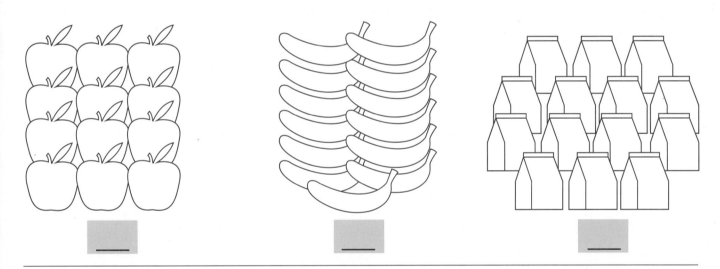

COLOR THE TWO PILES WITH THE SAME NUMBER OF ELEMENTS.

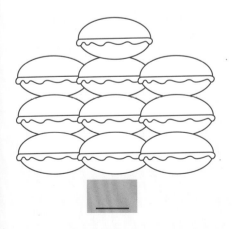 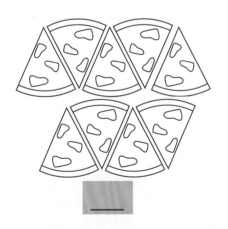 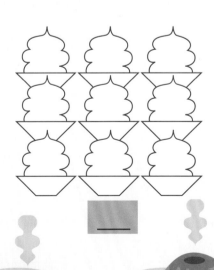

THE GREEDY MONSTER IS ALWAYS HUNGRY AND ALWAYS CHOOSES THE FULLEST PLATE. THIS IS WHY HE DIRECTS HIS MOUTH TO THE PLATE WITH THE BIGGER NUMBER OF ELEMENTS.

WHEN HE FINDS TWO EQUAL PLATES, HE HESITATES AND STOPS TO THINK...

COMPLETE WITH THE CORRECT NUMBER AND SYMBOL.

COUNT HOW MANY ELEMENTS THERE ARE ON EACH PLATE AND WRITE THE NUMBER IN THE BLANKS. THEN LOOK FOR THE APPROPRIATE SYMBOL AMONG THE STICKERS AND STICK THE SIGNS FOR "GREATER THAN," "LESS THAN," OR "IS EQUAL TO" BETWEEN THE PLATES.

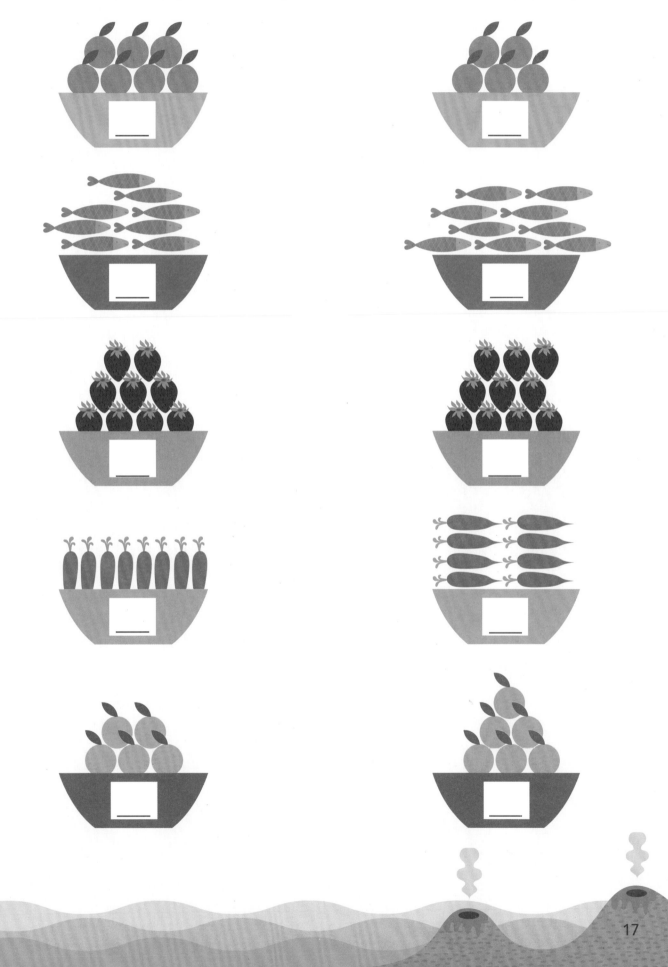

THE GREEDY MONSTER HAS EATEN SOME SNACKS!

CHOOSE THE CORRECT SHAPE FOR EACH SNACK AND COLOR IT IN, THEN LOOK FOR THE CORRECT PIECE AMONG THE STICKERS AND STICK IT TO COMPLETE THE SNACKS.

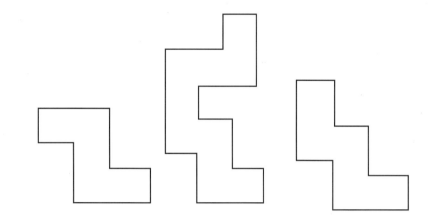

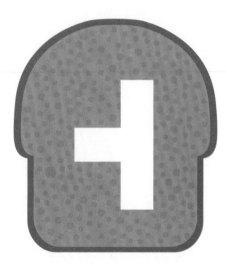
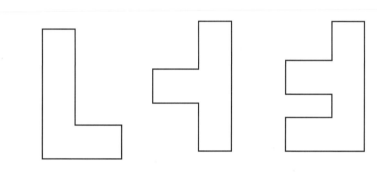

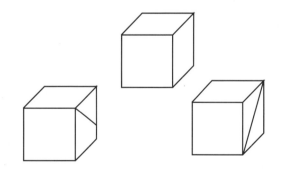

THERE'S MAIL!

Like most cities, Zot also has a post office. Postcards, letters, small and big packages are sorted, stamped and delivered by the postman monster and his helpers.

The postman is very accurate, fast and efficient, he only has one little flaw:

HE'S THE CRABBIEST MONSTER IN ALL OF ZOT!

If he gets angry, and this actually happens quite often, he sulks and starts doing everything the other way round: he delivers the mail to those who sent it, takes the stamps off the letters and starts saying the opposite of what he thinks!

When the postman monster gets angry, the whole office is thrown into turmoil: piles of packages out of place, bagfuls of swapped mail and other kinds of disasters follow one another while his helpers try to put everything back in place.

This morning, for example, all it took was a draft between his antennae for the postman monster to go mad and start mixing the incoming mail up, after it had already been sorted in alphabetical order!

He also sold the wrong stamps to those clients who wanted to send some mail and he mixed his helpers' bags up, so those poor monsters ended up in the right area with the wrong bag, one full of letters addressed elsewhere.

FIND OUT WHAT NUMBER THE POSTMAN MONSTER IS REALLY THINKING ABOUT.

REMEMBER: HE'S ANGRY, SO HE'S SAYING THE OPPOSITE OF WHAT IS IN HIS HEAD!

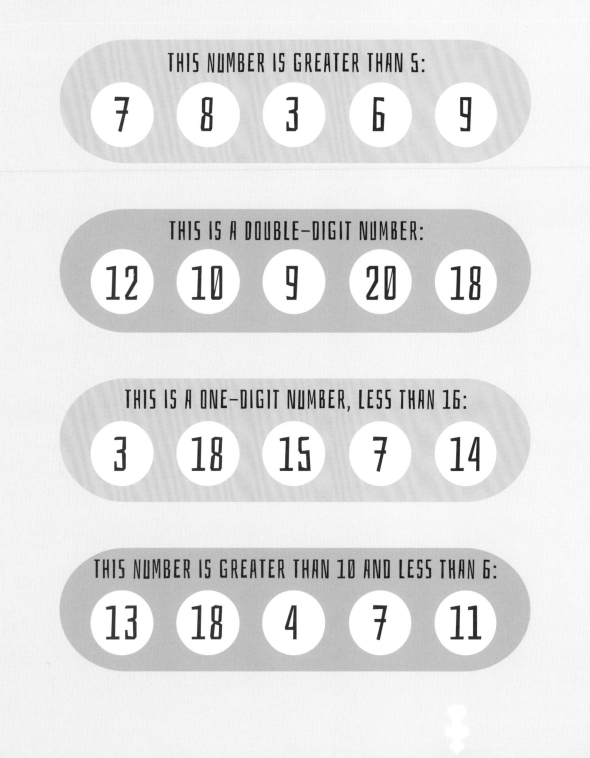

THIS NUMBER IS GREATER THAN 5:

7   8   3   6   9

THIS IS A DOUBLE-DIGIT NUMBER:

12   10   9   20   18

THIS IS A ONE-DIGIT NUMBER, LESS THAN 16:

3   18   15   7   14

THIS NUMBER IS GREATER THAN 10 AND LESS THAN 6:

13   18   4   7   11

21

COMPLETE THE ENVELOPES.

THERE'S SO MUCH TO DO AT THE POST OFFICE! WE MUST BE CAREFUL, ACCURATE AND TIDY AND... OH JEEZ, IT'S STARTING TO RAIN! POOR POSTMAN MONSTER, HE WANTED TO GO FOR A WALK! QUICK, HELP HIM FINISH HIS JOB BEFORE HE STARTS SULKING AND DOES EVERYTHING THE OTHER WAY ROUND!

BEFORE YOU START, STICK THE TOKEN STICKERS ON A THIN CARDBOARD AND CUT THEM OUT: THEY'LL HELP YOU WITH YOUR CALCULATIONS.

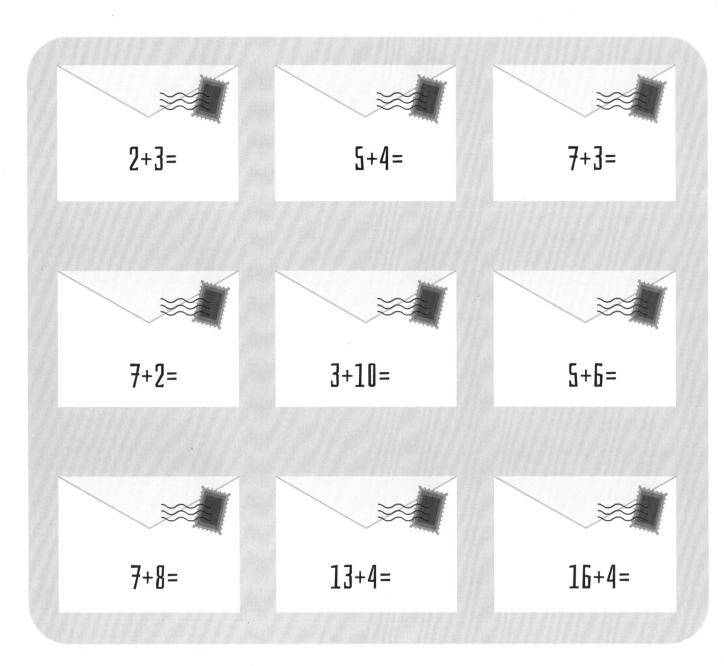

2+3=

5+4=

7+3=

7+2=

3+10=

5+6=

7+8=

13+4=

16+4=

THERE ARE BIG AND SMALL PACKAGES TO SORT OUT!

DO THE CALCULATIONS AND MARK THE PACKAGES BY COLORING IN THE LABEL ACCORDING TO THE KEY.

NUMBERS THAT ARE LESS THAN 6

NUMBERS BETWEEN 6 AND 10

NUMBERS THAT ARE GREATER THAN 10

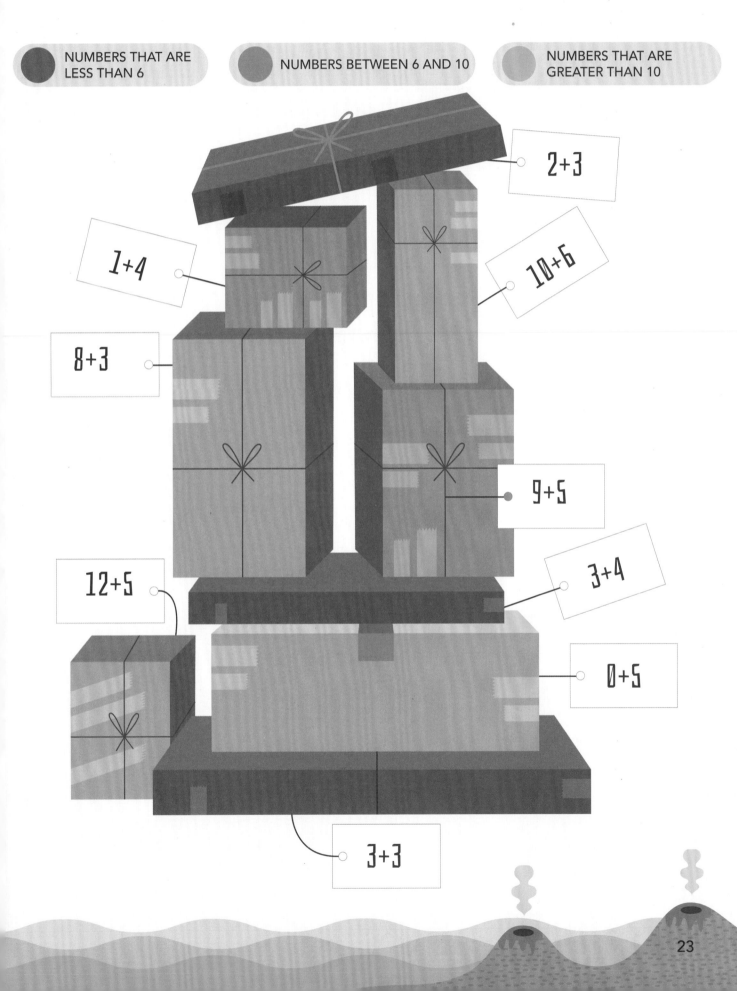

2+3

1+4

10+6

8+3

9+5

3+4

12+5

0+5

3+3

MATCH EACH ENVELOPE TO ITS STAMP,
SO THAT THE TWO NUMBERS ADD UP TO 10.

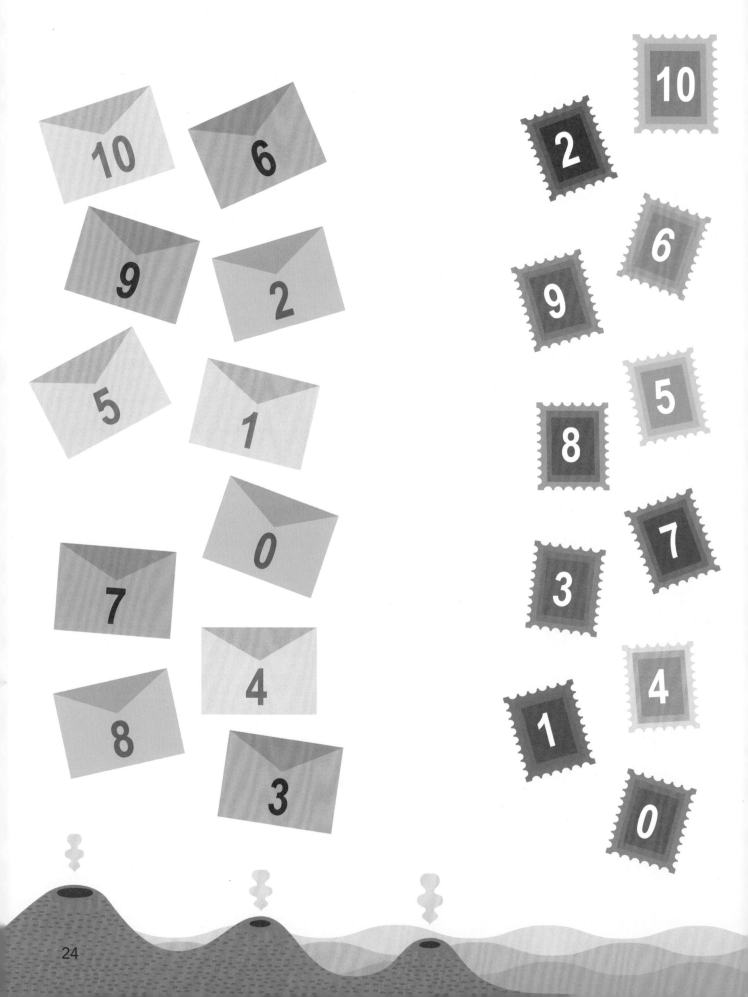

FIND AT LEAST THREE DIFFERENT WAYS TO GET THE NUMBER ON EACH STAMP, LIKE IN THE EXAMPLE.

6

3+3
5+
+

5

10

8

12

16

20

HELP THE POSTMAN MONSTER SOLVE THESE PROBLEMS. LOOK AT THE DRAWINGS.

THERE ARE 4 WHITE ENVELOPES IN THE POSTMAN'S BAG, 1 GREEN ENVELOPE AND 2 YELLOW ENVELOPES.
HOW MANY ENVELOPES ARE THERE IN THE BAG?

1

THE INBOX CONTAINS 7 POSTCARDS FROM THE BEACH, 3 FROM THE COUNTRYSIDE AND 5 FROM THE MOUNTAINS.
HOW MANY POSTCARDS ARE THERE OVERALL?

2

THE POSTMAN MONSTER DELIVERED 8 LETTERS THIS MORNING, 5 AT LUNCH TIME AND 6 IN THE AFTERNOON.
HOW MANY LETTERS DID HE DELIVER OVERALL?

3

ZIG ZAG HAS RECEIVED 7 LETTERS, SPYX HAS RECEIVED 2 LETTERS MORE THAN ZIG ZAG.

HOW MANY LETTERS HAS SPYX RECEIVED?

4

THE POSTMAN MONSTER AND HIS HELPER ARE DELIVERING THE POST. THE POSTMAN HAS DELIVERED 6 LETTERS, HIS HELPER HAS DELIVERED 3 MORE.

HOW MANY LETTERS HAVE BEEN DELIVERED OVERALL?

5

6

THE POSTMAN MONSTER DELIVERED:
THREE POSTCARDS ON MONDAY,
TWO PACKAGES ON TUESDAY,
ONE LETTER ON WEDNESDAY,
FOUR POSTCARDS ON THURSDAY,
TWO LETTERS ON FRIDAY,
ONE LETTER ON SATURDAY,
TWO PACKAGES ON SUNDAY.

HOW MANY THINGS DID HE DELIVER OVERALL?

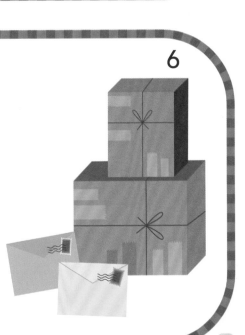

THE CLINIC

Maybe you've never thought about it. Maybe you think monsters are always strong and sturdy. Well, you're wrong.

MONSTERS ALSO GET SICK!

Even the yuckiest and smelliest swamp monster or the cruelest attic monster sometimes gets sick. Just yesterday, a monster was walking down the road and, despite having seven pairs of eyes, didn't see a manhole and, fa-thud, fell down, breaking three antennae. And last week, two little monsters were playing with a ball and tumbled down a hill, scraping all their knees.

In winter, feverish monsters, monsters with runny noses, hoarse monsters, and monsters with sore throats pack into the clinic. In the waiting room today there is a monster with a toothache, a monster with some strange blisters on his body, and one who fell from his stilts and broke half a dozen of his arms.

The doctor is very good: he knows remedies for every illness and injury, but he's also a very messy and untidy kind of monster. His grandma used to tell him that "each thing has its place and each place has its thing," but it seems like the doctor didn't learn this lesson.

Luckily, his helpers pick up, sort out, and tidy up his messes.

THERE ARE SO MANY MONSTERS IN THE WAITING ROOM!

CALCULATE THE RESULT OF THESE OPERATIONS, THEN PUT THE PATIENTS IN ORDER FROM THE HIGHEST TO THE LOWEST NUMBER BY WRITING THE NUMBER IN THE YELLOW DOT, AND FIND OUT IN WHAT ORDER THEY WILL BE VISITED.

$15 - 12 - 3 = ...$

$20 - 7 = ...$

$15 - 14 = ...$

$20 - 15 = ...$

$9 + 8 = ...$

$2 + 3 + 4 = ...$

$17 - 7 = ...$

$8 - 5 = ...$

$12 + 8 = ...$

$15 - 8 = ...$

THE DOCTOR IS QUITE FORGETFUL!

HE HAS FORGOTTEN THE NAMES OF THE PATIENTS THESE MEDICINES ARE FOR. HELP HIM MATCH EACH PATIENT TO THE RIGHT MEDICINE BY READING THE CLUES CAREFULLY.

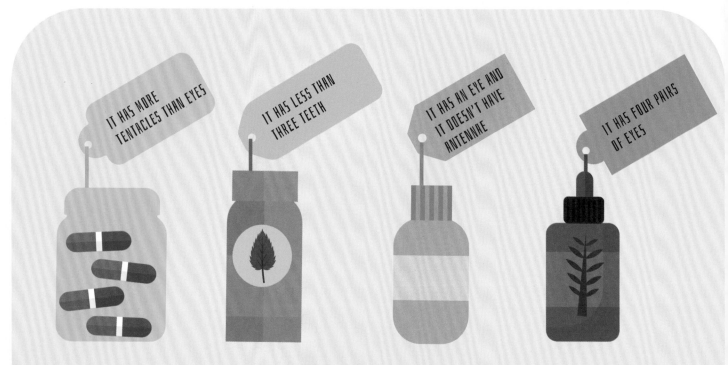

A SUGGESTION: READ ALL THE LABELS CAREFULLY BEFORE MATCHING THEM.

IT HAS TWO LEGS AND AN ODD NUMBER OF EYES

IT HAS MORE THAN THREE EYES

IT HAS THE SAME NUMBER OF EYES AND LEGS

IT'S FURRY

THIS CLUMSY MONSTER HAS TUMBLED DOWN THE STAIRS!

THIS POOR MONSTER HAS BROKEN SOME OF HIS ANTENNAE. CHOOSE A BAND-AID FROM THE STICKERS AND PUT IT ON ONE OF THE INJURED ANTENNAE: YOU CAN RECOGNIZE THEM BECAUSE THEY DISPLAY A FALSE EQUIVALENCE.

THE DOCTOR IS AS CLUMSY AS USUAL AND HAS LET SOME BANDAGES AND CREAMS FALL DOWN.

HELP HIM PUT EVERYTHING BACK! FOLLOW THE CHAIN OF OPERATIONS WRITTEN ON THE UNROLLED BANDAGES, THEN WORK OUT WHAT NUMBERS ARE HIDDEN UNDER THOSE SPOTS OF CREAM.

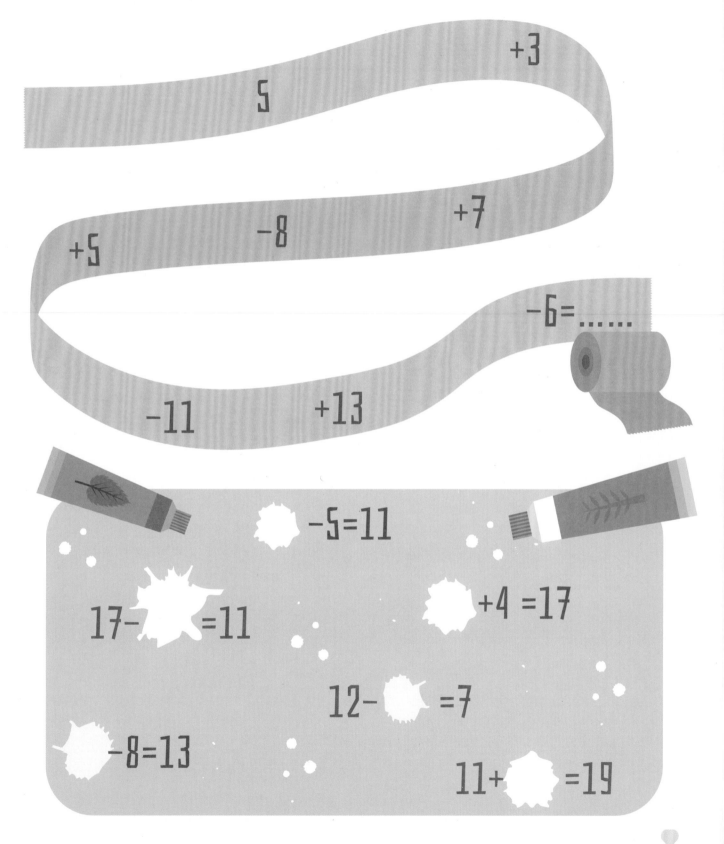

5

+3

+7

−8

+5

−6=.......

−11

+13

−5=11

17−⬤=11

⬤+4 =17

12−⬤=7

⬤−8=13

11+⬤=19

THIS HECTIC DAY AT THE CLINIC IS FINALLY OVER.

HELP THE DOCTOR TIDY THE CLINIC UP. COMPLETE THE LABELS ON THESE BOTTLES OF SYRUP, KEEPING IN MIND THAT EACH NUMBER IS THE SUM OF THE TWO NUMBERS BELOW IT.

THE DOCTOR IS DOING INVENTORY.

HELP HIM WORK OUT HOW MANY PIECES OF EACH PRODUCT HE HAS.

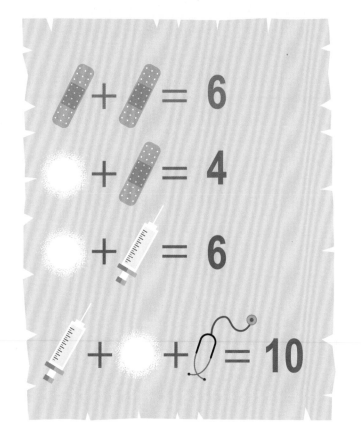

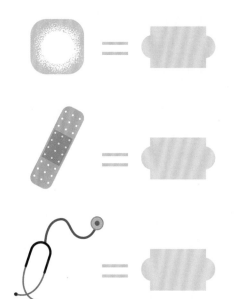

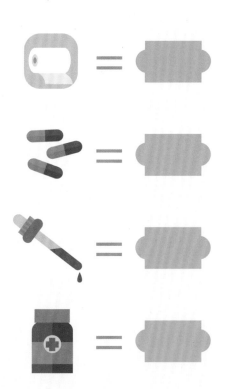

EUREKA!

A pencil in his hand, a notepad, a ruler, a pair of compasses, and a calculator in the other...

HERE'S THE INVENTOR MONSTER: THE MOST INGENIOUS OF ZOT'S INHABITANTS.

Ever since he was a child, he's always been taking stuff apart to put them back together in his own way. Like the time when he fixed a watering can on top of an umbrella: "What use does an umbrella have," he said, "when it's not raining? In this way, it's always raining!"

His parents were always worried when he shut himself in his room to design a new invention, especially after that time he altered the mixer and got raspberry jelly all over the living room. His friends, however, were eager to test his homework-popping machine, which automatically did the most boring homework.

Now that he's older, the inventor monster still has brilliant ideas, even if things often go wrong when he tries to put his projects into action.

THIS MACHINE IS LOSING SOME PIECES!

ALL THE GEARS HAVE DISAPPEARED! HELP THE INVENTOR PUT EACH GEAR BACK INTO ITS PLACE! LOOK FOR THEM AMONG THE STICKERS AT THE BACK OF THE BOOK AND STICK THEM ON THEIR CORRESPONDING WHITE OUTLINE.

THE INVENTOR MONSTER HAS INVENTED A NUMBER-SHOOTING MACHINE!

HE STILL NEEDS TO WORK OUT EXACTLY WHAT IT'S FOR, BUT IN THE MEANTIME IT HAS FILLED ZOT UP WITH NUMBERS! YOU CAN ALSO BUILD YOUR OWN NUMBER-SHOOTING MACHINE! USE THE STICKERS TO BUILD TWO BIG DICE, THEN TOSS THEM AND FIND OUT THE HIGHEST NUMBER YOU CAN GET WITH THOSE TWO FIGURES.

YOU CAN ALSO CHALLENGE A FRIEND: WHOEVER GETS THE HIGHEST NUMBER SCORES ONE POINT! USE THE TABLE BELOW TO MARK YOUR SCORES.

PLAYER 1	PLAYER 2

THE INVENTOR MONSTER HAS MODIFIED THE NUMBER-SHOOTING MACHINE!

IT'S NOT SHOOTING NUMBERS ANYMORE, BUT AN ORANGE TOKEN FOR EACH TEN AND A GREEN TOKEN FOR EACH UNIT. FOLLOW THE KEY TO FIND OUT WHAT NUMBERS THE MACHINE HAS COME UP WITH.

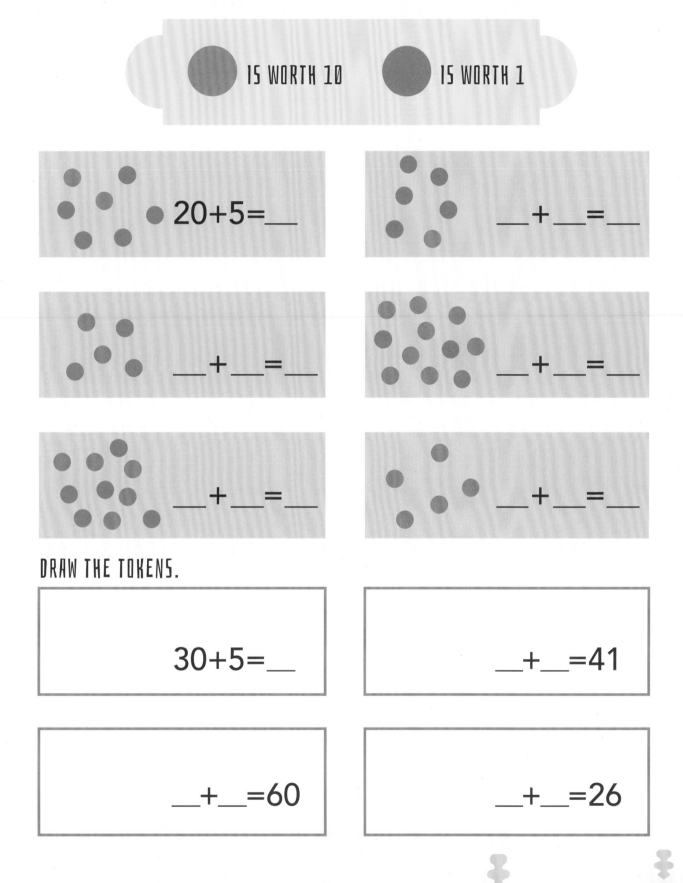

IS WORTH 10

IS WORTH 1

20+5=___

___+___=___

___+___=___

___+___=___

___+___=___

___+___=___

DRAW THE TOKENS.

30+5=___

___+___=41

___+___=60

___+___=26

39

IT'S RAINING TODAY IN ZOT AND THE MONSTERS ARE BORED. WHAT COULD THEY DO? DON'T WORRY! THE INVENTOR MONSTER IS HERE WITH ONE OF HIS INVENTIONS: THE RIDDLE-SHOOTING MACHINE.

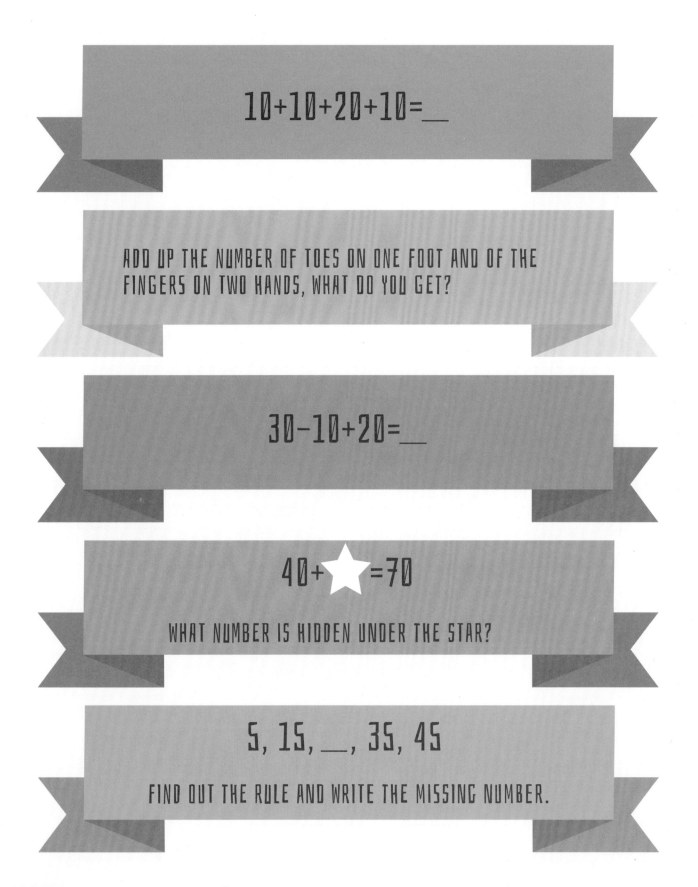

$10+10+20+10=\underline{}$

ADD UP THE NUMBER OF TOES ON ONE FOOT AND OF THE FINGERS ON TWO HANDS, WHAT DO YOU GET?

$30-10+20=\underline{}$

$40+\bigstar=70$

WHAT NUMBER IS HIDDEN UNDER THE STAR?

5, 15, $\underline{}$, 35, 45

FIND OUT THE RULE AND WRITE THE MISSING NUMBER.

THE MACHINE GOES ON SHOOTING EVEN MORE COMPLEX CONUNDRUMS.

I THINK ABOUT A NUMBER, I ADD 2 AND GET 5. WHAT WAS THE NUMBER?

I THINK ABOUT A NUMBER, I ADD 10 AND GET 18. WHAT WAS THE NUMBER?

I THINK ABOUT A NUMBER, I DEDUCT 5 AND GET 4. WHAT WAS THE NUMBER?

I THINK ABOUT A NUMBER, I DEDUCT 30 AND GET 20. WHAT WAS THE NUMBER?

I THINK ABOUT A NUMBER GREATER THAN 10 AND LESS THAN 20. THE SUM OF ITS DIGITS IS 4. WHAT IS THE NUMBER?

HELP! THE INVENTOR MONSTER'S MACHINES ARE OUT OF CONTROL TODAY! HE DOESN'T REMEMBER HOW TO TURN THEM OFF, BUT YOU CAN HELP HIM!

THE CAKE MACHINE HAS TOO MUCH SMOKE COMING OUT! TO TURN IT OFF, YOU NEED TO SOLVE THIS SUDOKU: EACH LINE AND COLUMN OF THE GRID MUST HAVE ALL THE COLORS SHOWN, WITHOUT REPEATING ANY.

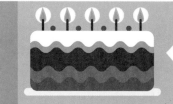

THE LAUNDRY MACHINE IS FILLING EVERYTHING UP WITH SOAP BUBBLES!

TO STOP IT, YOU NEED TO FIND THE RIGHT COMBINATION OF COLORS: EACH GRID MUST BE COMPLETED IN A SYMMETRICAL WAY, WITH THE RED LINE IN THE MIDDLE. LOOK AT THE EXAMPLE! IF YOU NEED MORE HELP, YOU CAN ALSO PUT A SMALL MIRROR ON THE RED LINE.

IS THE PARTY HERE?

As you might have guessed, a loud, lively racket reigns in Zot. Each monster does a different job and has a unique personality and tastes. But there is something, besides snack time, that all of Zot's inhabitants, from the most cheerful to the grumpiest, from the shyest to the chattiest, have in common.

EVERYONE, WITHOUT EXCEPTION, LOVES TO PARTY!

A party hat on their head (or heads!), a party horn in their mouth, and a piece of cake in their hand, as soon as the music starts they are all ready to dance, play games, and go wild.

Do you want to know what they've come up with to always have an excuse to celebrate? They invented the week-versary party, so there's no need to put everything back after a party as it's always time to plan a new one. It's brilliant, right?

WHO'S THE PARTY FOR TODAY?

READ THE CLUES AND FIND THE MONSTER.

BIT BOT

TUK

URSUS

LUCY

MOLLY

ZIG ZAG

CLUES

- THE PARTY IS FOR SOMEONE WITH MORE THAN ONE EYE
- HE OR SHE HAS AT LEAST TWO PAIRS OF ANTENNAE
- HE OR SHE IS NOT FURRY
- HE OR SHE DOESN'T HAVE TWO LEGS

THE PARTY IS FOR

_____

HELP LUCY GET EVERYTHING SHE NEEDS!

PREPARATIONS ARE HAPPENING! COMPLETE THE DRAWINGS, WRITE THE OPERATION AND CALCULATE.

5 GUESTS ARE COMING TO MY PARTY. I'M PREPARING 3 COLORFUL BALLOONS FOR EACH OF THEM. HOW MANY BALLOONS DO I NEED?

_____

   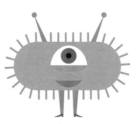

I WANT TO MAKE 6 CAKES AND I'LL PUT 5 STRAWBERRIES ON EACH OF THEM. HOW MANY STRAWBERRIES DO I NEED?

_____

 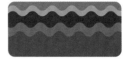

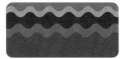 

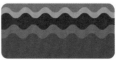 

46

I NEED 3 FORKS AND 2 GLASSES FOR EACH OF MY GUESTS (HAVING LOTS OF ARMS IS REALLY USEFUL!). HOW MANY DO I NEED TO BUY IN TOTAL?

_____

I'LL USE 4 FESTOONS TO DECORATE THE ROOM, WITH 8 FLAGS EACH. HOW MANY FLAGS WILL THERE BE IN TOTAL? AS I WILL ALTERNATE A GREEN AND A YELLOW FLAG, HOW MANY WILL THERE BE FOR EACH COLOR?

_____

HELP LUCY DECORATE THESE CAKES WITH STICKERS.

I HAVE 12 STRAWBERRIES AND I NEED TO DECORATE 6 PASTRIES, EACH WITH THE SAME NUMBER OF FRUIT. HOW MANY STRAWBERRIES ARE GOING TO BE ON EACH PASTRY?____

I HAVE 2 BASKETS AND I NEED TO PUT THE SAME AMOUNT OF SWEETS IN EACH OF THEM. I HAVE 8 LEMON-FLAVORED CANDIES, 6 CHOCOLATES, AND 4 LOLLY POPS.
HOW MANY CANDIES DO I PUT IN EACH BASKET?_____
HOW MANY CHOCOLATES?_____
HOW MANY LOLLY POPS?_____

ANSWERS

P. 5: CONNECT THE DOTS

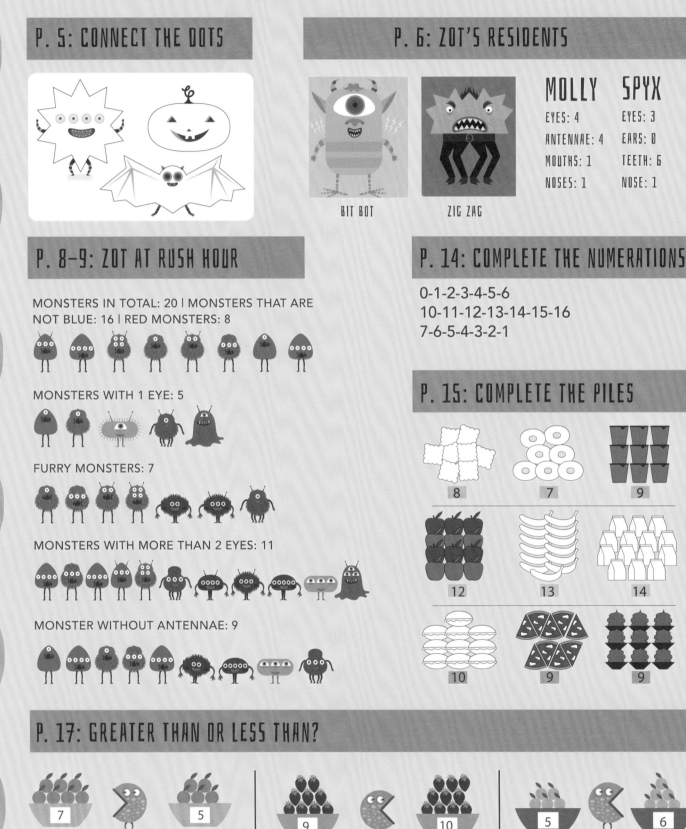

P. 6: ZOT'S RESIDENTS

BIT BOT

ZIG ZAG

MOLLY

EYES: 4
ANTENNAE: 4
MOUTHS: 1
NOSES: 1

SPYX

EYES: 3
EARS: 0
TEETH: 6
NOSE: 1

P. 8-9: ZOT AT RUSH HOUR

MONSTERS IN TOTAL: 20 | MONSTERS THAT ARE
NOT BLUE: 16 | RED MONSTERS: 8

MONSTERS WITH 1 EYE: 5

FURRY MONSTERS: 7

MONSTERS WITH MORE THAN 2 EYES: 11

MONSTER WITHOUT ANTENNAE: 9

P. 14: COMPLETE THE NUMERATIONS

0-1-2-3-4-5-6
10-11-12-13-14-15-16
7-6-5-4-3-2-1

P. 15: COMPLETE THE PILES

8   7   9

12   13   14

10   9   9

P. 17: GREATER THAN OR LESS THAN?

7   5   9   10   5   6

8   9   8   8

PP. 18-19: THE SNACKS' MISSING PIECES

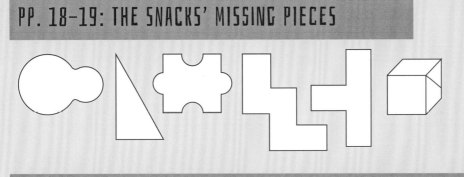

P. 21: THE ANGRY POSTMAN SAYS THE OPPOSITE OF WHAT HE'S THINKING

THIS NUMBER IS GREATER THAN 5: 3   ~~7~~ ~~8~~ 3 ~~6~~ ~~9~~

THIS IS A DOUBLE-DIGIT NUMBER: 9   12 ~~10~~ 9 ~~20~~ 18

THIS IS A ONE-DIGIT NUMBER, LESS THAN 16: 18   ~~3~~ 18 ~~15~~ ~~7~~ ~~14~~

THIS NUMBER IS GREATER THAN 10 AND LESS THAN 6: 7   ~~13~~ 18 ~~4~~ 7 11

P. 22: COMPLETE THE ENVELOPES

2+3=5   5+4=9   7+3=10

7+2=9   3+10=13   5+6=11

7+8=15   13+4=17   16+4=20

P. 23: BIG AND SMALL PACKAGES TO SORT OUT!

P. 24: MATCH EACH ENVELOPE TO ITS STAMP

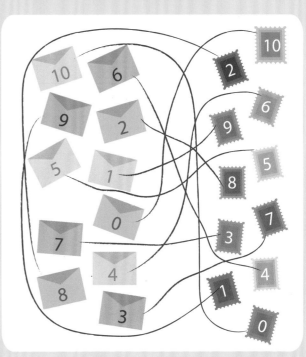

PP. 26–27: THE POSTMAN'S QUIZ

1) 7

3) 19

5) 9

2) 15

4) 9

6) 15

P. 29: QUEUING IN THE WAITING ROOM. WHO GETS SEEN FIRST?

12+8=20 ①
9+8=17 ②
20-7=13 ③
17-7=10 ④
2+3+4=9 ⑤
15-8=7 ⑥
20-15=5 ⑦
8-5=3 ⑧
15-14=1 ⑨
15-12-3=0 ⑩

P. 30:

PP. 30–31: THE FORGETFUL DOCTOR

IT HAS MORE TENTACLES THAN EYES

IT HAS LESS THAN THREE TEETH

IT HAS AN EYE AND IT DOESN'T HAVE ANTENNAE

IT HAS FOUR PAIRS OF EYES

P. 31:

IT HAS TWO LEGS AND AN ODD NUMBER OF EYES

IT HAS MORE THAN THREE EYES

IT HAS THE SAME NUMBER OF EYES AND LEGS

IT'S FURRY

P. 32: BROKEN ANTENNAE

13−5=12−7   7+4=10+1

7+7=16−2

5+8=3+9

10−3=5+3

17+3=12+8

P. 33: BANDAGES AND CREAMS

THE RESULT OF THE OPERATIONS ON THE BANDAGE IS 8

16 −5=11

17−6=11   13 +4 =17

21 −8=13   12−5 =7

11+ 8 =19

PP. 34−35: LET'S SORT THE CLINIC OUT

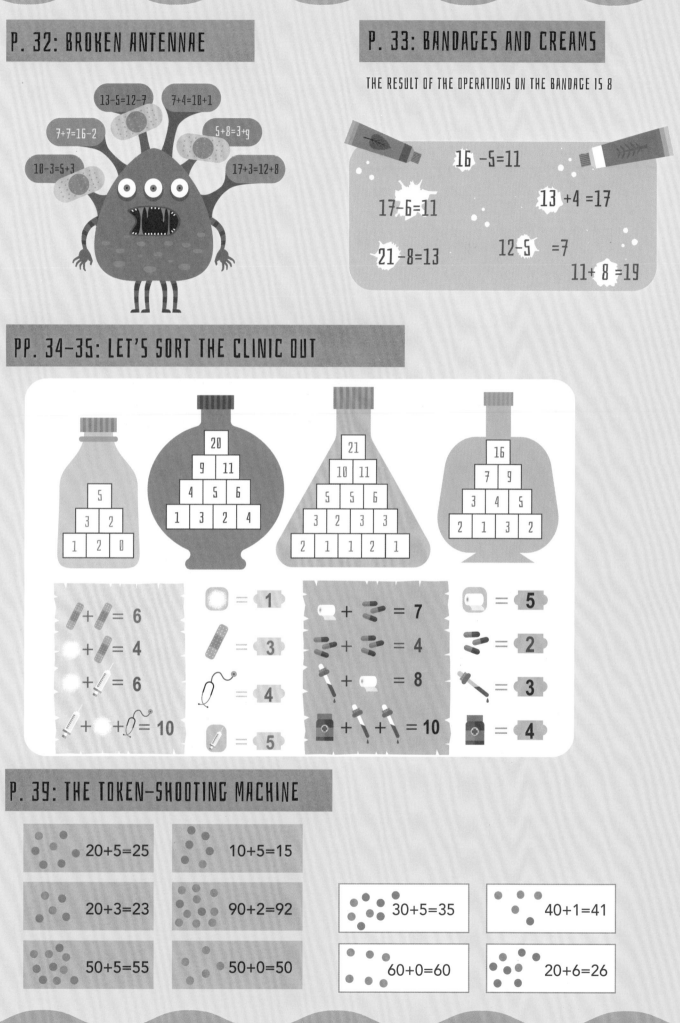

5
3 2
1 2 0

20
9 11
4 5 6
1 3 2 4

21
10 11
5 5 6
3 2 3 3
2 1 1 2 1

16
7 9
3 4 5
2 1 3 2

+ = 6
+ = 4
+ = 6
+ + = 10

= 1
= 3
= 4
= 5

+ = 7
+ = 4
+ = 8
+ + = 10

= 5
= 2
= 3
= 4

P. 39: THE TOKEN−SHOOTING MACHINE

20+5=25   10+5=15

20+3=23   90+2=92

50+5=55   50+0=50

30+5=35   40+1=41

60+0=60   20+6=26

53

PP. 40—41: THE RIDDLE-SHOOTING MACHINE

10+10+20+10=50

ADD UP THE NUMBER OF TOES ON ONE FOOT AND OF THE FINGERS ON TWO HANDS, WHAT DO YOU GET? 15

30-10+20=40

40+30=70

5, 15, 25, 35, 45

I THINK ABOUT A NUMBER, I ADD 2 AND GET 5. WHAT WAS THE NUMBER? 3

I THINK ABOUT A NUMBER, I ADD 10 AND GET 18. WHAT WAS THE NUMBER? 8

I THINK ABOUT A NUMBER, I DEDUCT 5 AND GET 4. WHAT WAS THE NUMBER? 9

I THINK ABOUT A NUMBER, I DEDUCT 30 AND GET 20. WHAT WAS THE NUMBER? 50

I THINK ABOUT A NUMBER GREATER THAN 10 AND LESS THAN 20. THE SUM OF ITS DIGITS IS 4. WHAT WAS THE NUMBER? 13

PP. 42—43: THE CAKES AND LAUNDRY MACHINE

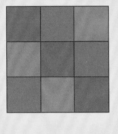
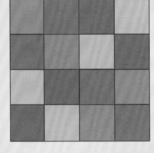
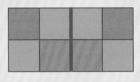
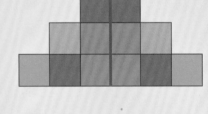
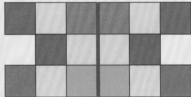

P. 45: THE PARTY IS FOR...

...LUCY!

PP. 46-47: PARTY PREPARATIONS

5 GUESTS ARE COMING TO MY PARTY. I'M PREPARING 3 COLORFUL BALLOONS FOR EACH OF THEM. HOW MANY BALLOONS DO I NEED? 3+3+3+3+3= 15

I WANT TO MAKE 6 CAKES AND I'LL PUT 5 STRAWBERRIES ON EACH OF THEM. HOW MANY STRAWBERRIES DO I NEED? 5+5+5+5+5+5= 30

I NEED 3 FORKS AND 2 GLASSES FOR EACH OF MY GUESTS (HAVING LOTS OF ARMS IS REALLY USEFUL!). HOW MANY DO I NEED TO BUY IN TOTAL? 5+5+5+5+5= 25

I'LL USE 4 FESTOONS TO DECORATE THE ROOM, WITH 8 FLAGS EACH. HOW MANY FLAGS WILL THERE BE IN TOTAL? AS I WILL ALTERNATE A GREEN AND A YELLOW FLAG, HOW MANY WILL THERE BE FOR EACH COLOR?
TOTAL NUMBER OF FLAGS: 8+8+8+8= 32
16 YELLOW FLAGS AND 16 GREEN ONES

PP. 48-49: LET'S DECORATE THE DESSERTS FOR THE PARTY

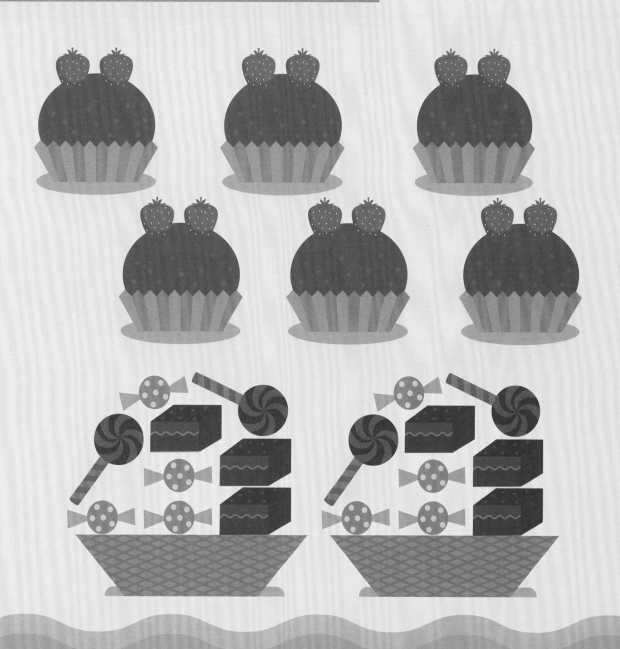

LINDA BERTOLA

A graduate in Foreign Languages for Intercultural Mediation at Milan's Università Cattolica, Linda Bertola is a linguistic and learning facilitator. She focuses on teaching and learning supports for pupils with special educational needs, working both in and out of school. She is also specialized in teaching Italian as a foreign language to children, teenagers and adults. She has collaborated with schools and associations as an intercultural teacher. She is passionate about teaching mathematics and making learning fun.

AGNESE BARUZZI

Agnese has a degree in Graphic Design from ISIA (Higher Institute for Artistic Industries) in Urbino. Since 2001, she has worked as an illustrator and author: she has made several works for young people in Italy, the United Kingdom, Japan, Portugal, the United States, France and Korea. She carries out workshops for children and adults in schools and libraries, and collaborates with agencies and graphic and editorial studios. In recent years, she has illustrated several titles for White Star Kids.

Copyright © 2022 Linda Bertola. All rights reserved.

Published by DragonFruit, an imprint of Mango Publishing, a division of Mango Publishing Group, Inc.

Mango is an active supporter of authors' rights to free speech and artistic expression in their books. Thank you in advance for respecting our authors' rights. For permission requests, please contact the publisher at:
Mango Publishing Group
2850 Douglas Road, 4th Floor
Coral Gables, FL
33134 USA
info@mango.bz

For special orders, quantity sales, course adoptions and corporate sales, please email the publisher at sales@mango.bz. For trade and wholesale sales, please contact Ingram Publisher Services at customer.service@ingramcontent.com or +1.800.509.4887.

Mad for Math: Become a Monster at Mathematics
ISBN: (p) 978-1-68481-045-1
BISAC: JNF035030, JUVENILE NONFICTION / Mathematics / Arithmetic

WHITE STAR KIDS

White Star Kids® is a registered trademark property of White Star s.r.l.

© 2019 White Star s.r.l.
Piazzale Luigi Cadorna, 6
20123 Milan, Italy
www.whitestar.it

Translation and Editing: Langue&Parole, Milan (Margaret Greenan)

All rights reserved. No part of this publication may be reproduced, stored in a retrieval system or transmitted in any form or by any means, electronic, mechanical, photocopying, recording or otherwise, without written permission from the publisher.

ISBN 978-88-544-1373-3
1 2 3 4 5 6   23 22 21 20 19

Printed in China

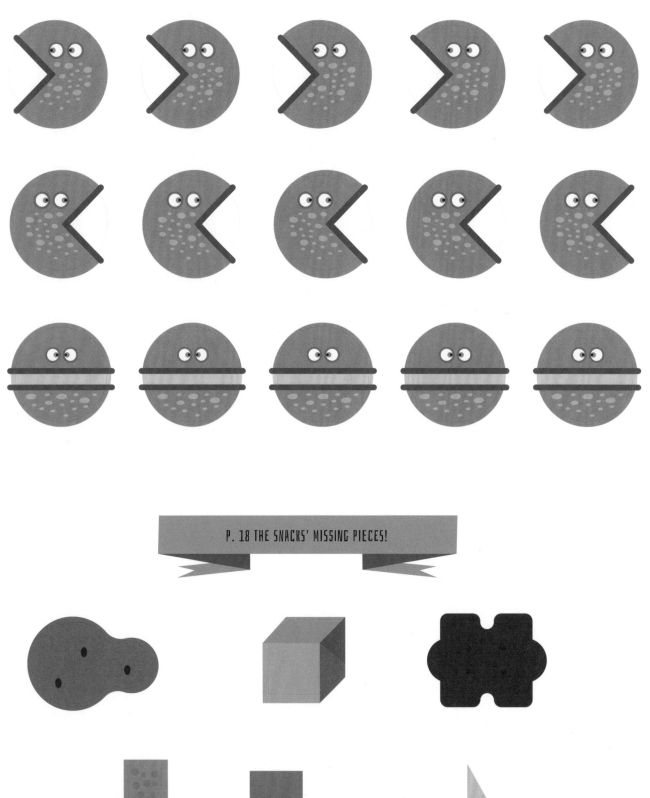